11/93

Windsongs AND Rainbows

Windsongs <u>AND</u> Rainbows

BY BURTON ALBERT · ILLUSTRATED BY SUSAN STILLMAN

SIMON & SCHUSTER BOOKS FOR YOUNG READERS
Published by Simon & Schuster   Z1450
New York • London • Toronto • Sydney • Tokyo • Singapore

SIMON & SCHUSTER BOOKS FOR YOUNG READERS
Simon & Schuster Building, Rockefeller Center
1230 Avenue of the Americas, New York, New York 10020

SIMON & SCHUSTER BOOKS FOR YOUNG READERS is a trademark of Simon & Schuster.
Designed by Lucille Chomowicz.
The text for this book was set in 16 point Usherwood Medium.
The illustrations were done in acrylic paint.
Manufactured in the United States of America 10 9 8 7 6 5 4 3 2 1

Library of Congress Cataloging-in-Publication Data
Albert, Burton. Windsongs and rainbows / by Burton Albert ; illustrated by Susan
Stillman.   p.   cm.   Summary: A rainstorm comes gently, grows in strength, and
gives way to the sun.   [1. Rain and rainfall—Fiction.   2. Storms—Fiction.]
I. Stillman, Susan, ill.   II. Title.   PZ7.A318Wi 1993   [E]—dc20   92-12012   CIP
ISBN: 0-671-76004-1

To Phil and Tina for all those wonderful seasons we've tasted and relished.   B.A.

For Laura and Daniel with all my love.   S.S.

ear the wind
spin the pinwheels
and flap the flag.
Rattle the shutters
and slam the door.
Rustle the leaves,
tinkle the chimes,
and gently creak the rocking chairs.

Feel the wind
nudge the boat
and tousle your hair.
Tug at the kite
and bob the balloons.
Flip your umbrella,
push at your back,
and spray the mist upon your face.

See the wind
snake the line
and ripple the waters.
Tease the embers
and curl the smoke.
Swirl the sand,
bend the reeds,
and churn the stormy clouds of gray.

H ear the rain
spatter your cap
and slap your slicker.
Thump the awnings
and rumble the spouts.
Splatter the cars,
wet the wipers,
and shower the dusty streets in sheets.

Feel the rain
tingle your toes
and soften the grass.
Muddy the trail
and wash your galoshes.
Dampen the bars,
smoothen the slide,
and tickle the cup of your upraised hand.

See the rain
pock the soil
and freckle the walk.
Pluck the roses
and pearl the web.
Huddle the ducks,
puddle the paths,
and color the sky with rainbows.

Sense the calm
caress the beach
and tease the breeze.
Await the wave
and echo the horn.
Greet the gulls,
scurry the pipers,
and muffle the dip of the dingy's oar.

Feel the sun
heat the pebbles
and dry the steps.
Toast your toes
and parch the tar.
Heat the hammock,
warm the shadows,
and sprint its glints across your eyes.

See the sun
pierce the clouds
and splay its rays.
Etch the trees
and darken the pelican.
Redden its center,
halo its orange,
and deepen the blues till wisp-of-moon.